Chapter 1

Three encounter the same day

I feel compelled to write from a different perspective after reading so many stories on the platform.Since most of the stories are based in Nigeria, I'm adding something Ugandan, which comes from deep in East Africa.

I'm James, and I'm from Kampala, Uganda, which is in East Africa. I'm a devoted reader of your blog.

As any African living in Africa is aware, being gay in our society is treated with caution and secrecy to the point where, when meeting new people in Kampala, we frequently use aliases rather than real names.

I was all about meeting gay men like me in 2018, when I had just discovered my sexuality and was exploring.The majority were men from Facebook, which at the time had more than 3,000 followers, and some were recommended by friends and fuck buddies.

I was all about maximizing my sexual desires to the fullest because in this country, you will be guaranteed a rematch if you do a good job sexually.By reading articles, watching gay porn, and testing my knowledge and skills on my partners, I went all the way out.I made it my mission to be unstoppable.

As requests and offers from men kept coming in from all directions, my phone was constantly ringing incessantly.Even though I had a lot of libido, I made sure I wasn't careless with my money.I chose carefully and never traveled a great distance.I kept my company in Kampala.

To be honest, the suburb I live in, Nakawa, was rather uninteresting.I lived next door to a gay neighbor, but I didn't like him sexually, so we stayed friends and sent each other connections for hookups.

This good day, I got a good lead from Facebook, which is the best place to find someone and far superior to Grinder.On this side of Africa, Grinder is where thieves, liars, kitos, and con artists are found.) He asked me to get in touch with Umar early that morning.

Umar and I first connected via Facebook two years ago, and we have kept in touch ever since.He would, on the other hand, act as though he had no idea what I was talking about whenever I tried to bring up gay conversations or ask for a hookup.

However, I must say that Umar is a very attractive individual.He has light skin, which is unusual for East Africans, and I could swear he wasn't a virgin despite his warm personality, polite demeanor, and "innocent" appearance.I didn't feel unsafe when I saw his invitation that morning because we had already established a strong friendship over time. As a result, I was happy to come over and fuck him.

I washed up quickly and took a Boda, also known as a motorcycle, to Kireka, where he was located. Since it was roughly 8 a.m., I arrived on time.He wanted us to get right to business because he was already dressed for work and didn't want to be late.He started touching me up and making sexy moans before I even had a chance to settle down.

We started kissing, but I followed his pace because it was so fast.I wanted to suck his nipple, eat his hole, and do all sorts of wickedly sweet things to him as we kissed like hungry animals.He just didn't want it, though.He wanted to be straight up sucked in!!!!!!

He got a condom, put it on my throbbing, 8-inch, rock-hard penis, lubricated our cooking utensils, and then turned around and led my cock into his hole on his own.

Because it wasn't hard to get into his man-pussy, he wasn't a virgin, as I had suspected.With each push, my dick just slowly got deeper and deeper into his warm, moist hole.

"Daddy fuck me... fuck my ass," he ordered, as he began to push his ass back into me once I was completely enclosed.

I jumped into action right away.After positioning his ass so that his hole was clearly visible, I began to sell him like a freed slave.

Umar's gentle nature vanished completely.As he rocked his bum-bum to match my merciless smashing, he became a complete cock-hungry slut, whining his waist and acting like he was possessed or something.Unfortunately, however, his boss answered the phone.It turned out that the office needed his attention right away, so he had to leave.Even though we did not cum, I was still as horny as a fuck as ever!!!!

As he literally dashed off to work, he gave me a kiss that said "till next time" and a thumbs up for a "job well done."

I made my way to the intersection where I could get a ride back home, still sexually frustrated.My phone vibrated to a notification as I waited for a vehicle.A friend by the name of Sammy had sent me a Facebook notification informing me that he wanted to meet me.

Sammy and I have been talking for some time, just like Umar, but he hasn't agreed to meet with me.He was short (about 5 feet 3 inches), had light skin (unlike Umar), and a very pretty face and smile.Additionally, Sammy was undoubtedly not Kenyan based on his features.I figured it must have been my lucky day because all of my crushes were automatically horny for my meat at the same time, and who was I to say no?

The sun had already begun to burn hot around 10 a.m.From Kireka, where I am currently located, to Kyambogo, Banda, where he is located, there was really no direct route other than a four-kilometer walk or several connecting transportation rides (which would probably cost me a lot of money that I did not have).Sammy had advised me to take my time because his brother, with whom he shared a home, was leaving that morning at 11 a.m., so I didn't have to rush.

I stood up and started walking.Yes, in order to get some good ass, I walked approximately four kilometers in the scorching sun.My mind was making up all the bad things I would do to him as I walked to his place, which gave me both energy and cock.This was the definitive answer to my prayers, as I had a persistent desire to ejaculate.

He was already waiting for me when I got there.He turned on the air conditioning, offered me a cold drink because he saw that I was weathered, and offered to hang my wet shirt.He was so adorable.

We stopped talking after a while and stared at each other in silence.Why are you gazing at me in that way?He asked hesitantly.I just couldn't help myself because he was absolutely fine.I instructed him to get closer so that I could explain why.I gave him a kiss and held his face in my hands as he got closer to me.

Sammy showed me that even though I thought I knew how to kiss, I was still learning.My cock grew so hard that I feared it would fall off my waist as he kissed my tongue and lips in such a way that I felt helpless and weak.

All I can remember is him kissing me while he was astride me on the sofa and taking off my singlet.I have no idea when or how we both got completely naked.

I kept wondering where he had been my whole life as we kissed and held hands because the passion was so strong and intense.

We did everything we could to each other.It was like magic when he took my dick in his mouth.He was good, and I mean "very good" when I say "good."

I stopped him, laid him on his back, and began licking every inch of his body as he shivered and called my name because I didn't want to get too close to his sucking.When I reached his sex den, I was captivated by what I saw.I had to do the necessary because it was so fresh and beautiful, like his entire body.Before savoring its full sweetness, I parted his supple, bouncy cheeks and inhaled the divine scent.By the time I was done, I didn't need any lube to enter him.Already, his hole was extremely soft and wet.

I had to force myself to stop Cumming as soon as I entered him.He was extremely, exceedingly sweet.

As I entered and exited him, we continued to kiss.

Our sex, in contrast to Umar's, was characterized by divine connection and stars.

We stopped kissing at one point and just stared at each other for what seemed like an eternity.No words were said.We only felt the beautiful passion and energy we were both experiencing.I reached for his bulky dick and began stroking it with its own juice, as if I could read his mind.

As I slowly rubbed his smooth thick cock while concentrating on the fat dick head, which seemed to be very sensitive because he would jerk and gasp whenever I did a palm rotation on it, I watched his beautiful face engulf in ecstasy.I continued doing this gently while simultaneously pushing my cock deeper into his moist tight tunnel and kissing his lovely lips at intervals.

He began to gently grunt as his eyes became teary after what seemed to be a brief moment of floating through space.I was certain he was about to cum at that point because he kept repeating my name.All of my barriers were torn down by the sight of him in such a good mood, and I found that I could no longer contain myself as I too began to feel my explosion approaching like a hurricane.

As my cock gave up all of the sperm in its possession, my mouth screamed and my entire body seemed to explode into a million stars.When his dick began to violently pulsate in my moist hands, I was still shaking from pure joy.As his ass hole tenderly extracted the last drop of my seed, thick cum melted all over my hands.

He went in and out of my slowly depleting dick while I was still catching my breath and began to slowly rotate his waist.

I was loving every moment of it because he was truly a sex god.I was surprised to see that we had been flirting for more than an hour when I checked the time.

We were worn out as we lay in each other's arms, but we refused to let go.My dick was already full from the amount of deliciousness it had just consumed, so I wished I could start a second round right away.

Sammy cooked us both a meal and we shared it after we had both washed.We cuddled as we watched television, and for the first time, I felt a strong desire to want such a life—one in which I could live with the love of my life and remain committed to him for the rest of my life—under one roof.

He wanted the mood to last as long as I did, but I had to go back to my place.

We spent more than 30 minutes kissing at his door before I left.We were unable to let go.

I was chatting with Sammy all the way home and when I got to where I wanted to go.

When I got home, I was completely worn out from walking four kilometers in the sweltering heat and from the massive ejaculation that came with over an hour of making love.I was drained.

Martins' phone buzzed just as I thought I had had enough for the day.

I have a "friends with benefits" relationship with Martins.He had dark skin and a thick, full, salt-and-pepper beard that matched his thick brow perfectly.The "benefit" of our friendship was that he supported me financially while I supported him sexually. He was much older than I was.Martins keeps a low profile, and I can guarantee that I am the only person with whom he has gay sex.Even though he is tall, we only saw each other occasionally."Save me from death, please."He sent a message.

I asked him in a state of panic, and his response made me laugh and roll my eyes.

He replied, "I am dying of horniness."

I asked him to come over to my place in Nakawa because we hadn't seen each other in a long time and I was certain that he would be extremely generous to me. He was overjoyed.

I began my preparations right away.I didn't have much to worry about because Martins had a dick that was medium in size.

A brief knock on my door followed shortly thereafter.The one was him.

Martins does not have a romantic sexual side.When he's horny, he usually acts aggressively and impatiently.

When he started kissing and rough-squeezing my dick, he had just entered my room.As if his clothes were infested with termites and ferocious ants, he hurriedly removed them.Before he opened his wallet and pulled out a condom, he only briefly sucked on me.I started positioning myself because I thought he wanted to fuck me;only to have him give me the condom and ask me to use it.My dick was miraculously stiff at this point.

Martins quickly climbed on top of me and began shoving my dick into his extremely tight hole.Getting my penis into Martins' ass was really frustrating for both of us, and it was obvious that Martins hadn't had sex in forever.But at some point, he was able to steal all of my meat from his man-oven, and then he started to ride me like he was under the influence of something. Until I closed my eyes and imagined that Sammy was riding me, I wasn't enjoying the sex, at which point the energy and desire came.He started to groan and growl like a monster as a huge load of sperm flew out of his cock and sprayed my face and chest as I held his thick waist and

began slamming hard and furiously into his hole.I was surprised that he did not masturbate in front of cum."Just like that," he showed up.
He was also strangling and suffocating my dick with his already very tight and nearly virgin ass hole, as his entire body stiffened viciously from the intense sensational shock he was experiencing from ejaculating.I immediately started pouring my juice into the condom.
"wow... how did you do that?"After he had recovered from his spasm, he inquired.He also found it hard to believe that he had let go without masturbating.
I told him it was a secret and laughed.If only he had known that I was thinking of someone else I had just fucked a few hours earlier, which is why I was able to maintain an erection for him.
He changed into his costume now that he was very content, and his generosity this time was shocking.I still had more than enough to keep, as well as enough to pay my rent and numerous other bills.He (Martins) still marvels at his ability to cum without touching himself, while I still wonder how I managed to keep up with three encounters in one day.

Chapter 2

My childhood lover

Faruq was my neighbor when I was a kid.Even though Faruq was a complete jerk, he was remarkable for having a big dick.And by "big," I mean that he has a very large, fat dick.
He was extremely sexually perverse as a teenager.I remember vividly how he would usually whip out his dick publicly and swing it for girls in our neighbourhood just to make them scream and run away.
We frequently hung out together despite the fact that he was older than I was and was more like my older brother's friend.
I was also a teenager at the time who had not yet fully comprehended his sexuality.Nevertheless, I already had an unconscious attraction to men, particularly Faruq.To tell you the truth, aside from wanting to grow up quickly, the primary reason I hung out with my older brother and his crew was to see Faruq's genitalia.
I would secretly hope that he would pull out his cock so I could see it every time we got together.
Faruq, the only son, lived with his mother and two sisters. His actions brought a great deal of shame to his family.Sadly, rather than scolding Faruq, his mother will defend him and fight back when mothers come to their house to pick a fight with Faruq's mother over his indecent exposure to their daughters.
I met Faruq for the first time while I was watching a movie at his house one day.I had gone with my older brother, but he had to leave me behind because of a girl.I had to wait for him to return so that we could go home together, but if we didn't, my parents would be furious and ask questions.
During my wait, a number of events occurred.
Faruq had started talking about how he was so horny and felt like fucking while we were watching a movie.As he spoke, he kept rubbing his dick, and it was clear that he wanted me to look at what he was doing. As a fan of big meat, I felt hopelessly taken in by the bait and looked at his rapidly expanding crotch.I couldn't look away from what he was doing; I couldn't.
He surprised me by bringing out his now-slightly hard monster and beginning to stroke it vigorously.His cock grew in size and length like something out of a movie, and I watched in awe. FARUQ's penis was extremely large!
He started talking about how he likes it when someone else does his masturbation for him."It is much sweeter when someone rubs your dick for you," he said, exacting his words.
He asked me to come and flirt with him, and I'm not sure what I said in response.Because I was thinking of so many things, I was initially hesitant and afraid.To begin, it was one thing to be drawn to something, but it was quite another to be brave enough to indulge in it.

"Come and play with my dick," he cooed in a seductive manner while repeatedly jerking his massive cock as if to inform me that it was his penis doing the invitation.
I felt my heart racing as I saw my hands reach for his pole. As soon as I touched his throbbing member, I knew I had finally found the missing piece of my life's puzzle, and that "missing piece" was BIG PENIS without a shadow of a doubt.
There would be no going back.
As I held the scalding, hot meat in my hand, my mind went blank with wonder.It was huge and long, and at that moment, I realized that the rumors about girls refusing to have sex with him weren't true after all.
He reached out his hands to the corner of his bed's head in complete awe and grabbed a bottle of pears baby oil. As he said, "make me happy," the oil smeared on his everlasting inches.
As I watched his face react to the magic my hand was doing to his cock, I started stroking him.I was thrilled to learn that I was to blame for the sweet sensation Faruq was experiencing because he truly had a banging pleasure face."do you love stroking my big dick?," he began to groan while raising his hips to meet my hand motion.He questioned me as I rubbed his monster all the way to the top and slowly took it down.
"Yeah," I managed to respond, despite my choked voice.
"Yes, I understand that you want to do this every day.Right?"As he asked, he gasped.
I replied, "If you want."My voice barely came across.
"Maybe I'll let you suck it the next time... would you like to do that?"As I gently squeezed the large cock head, he groaned.
I was able to respond with "Okay."
I nodded when he asked if my dick was hard.
He encouraged, "Feel free to wank yourself," and I quickly pulled out my dripping cock and began to stroke myself with one hand while holding on to his fuck stick with the other.
He instructed, "Let me see you stroke your dick;"As a result, I positioned myself so that he could observe my happiness.
He asked me to raise my shirt and get closer to him as I pleased both of our members, which I did.When Faruq took one of my nipples in his mouth, I experienced nipple stimulation for the first time in my life—the only sexual experience I knew of was on my dick—and fresh fireworks exploded in my head.
He started getting intense on my nipple at that moment. He gently bit it, used this tongue to tickle it, and sucked it seriously while using his other hand to play with my other nipple. The excitement made me tremble and shake.

I couldn't control myself because I was completely out of my mind and started saying all kinds of sweet things.As I felt my ejaculation surge toward my dick hole like a hurricane, I started to go into and out of severe shock.
He put his fingers on my lips and, with a big grin on his face, whispered "shhh" as I started to scream.He adored the fact that I was in pure bliss.
He grunted, "wank me faster baby,,, faster," "wank this big dick faster baby," "make daddy happy," "make me cum baby," "show me you love it," and "wank me baby."Because I was

rapidly approaching my zenith, it was nearly impossible for me to hear him, but I managed to do as he instructed.

As he grabbed my face and gave me the kiss of my life, his body began to stiffen quickly.He sucked my lips with his warm tongue, passionately searching my soul, and made me soar to the clouds.

As we began to simultaneously melt our juices in my two hands, we grunted like beasts.I kept stroking us because I couldn't control myself. In fact, I had brought our cum dripping cocks together and started stroking them together, which was excruciatingly intense.We both jerked simultaneously to avoid being electrocuted until the sensation subsided.

Faruq gave me a brief, deep kiss before asking me to brush his sperm-covered dick with my mouth.I did it without thinking twice.I wiped everything off until his cock was spotless.

He moaned, "Oh yeah...that's my boy," as I squeezed his cock to remove any residue.

He assured us, "Don't worry, I won't tell your brother or anyone," after we had finished cleaning up.

Since he was the one who initiated everything, his statement caught me off guard, but I didn't say anything.I simply left with a nod.

The following day, while my brother and his friends were playing games in his room, we had the same incident in his mother's bedroom.He secured our rooms so that no one could enter.

My brother called his name, but he refused to answer as we kissed and I stroked him off to climax.While he used the door, I sneaked out through the backyard window after we were done.We were unseen.

I started becoming envious of him whenever I saw him and my brother and their group of friends seduce girls over time.He was aware that I was seriously developing feelings.When his eyes would occasionally catch mine, he would become icy and withdraw.

We started fighting, and during one of our fights, he asked me what I wanted from him. I told him that I needed his time, and he did as I asked, which surprised me.

Because he wanted to spend time with me, he started avoiding his friends by making excuses for his absence.

We began meeting in public places outside of our neighborhood because of prying eyes.

He informed me that I would be sucking and swallowing him the following day, one day after I had finished wanking him off and he had sucked my both nipples, making them sore.I can usually get ready before he usually gives notice.

I could barely sleep that day because I was so excited.To ensure that I prepared my throat for his monster, I even practiced with a cucumber.

We met the following day at his house, in his mother's room, and I fell to my knees in praise.

I was so disappointed that I was unable to take him the way I wanted because, regrettably, his penis was too big for my mouth.He cheered me up and assured me that since it was my first attempt, I would improve over time. He saw that I was hopeless.

He held my head back while wanking over my open, thirsty mouth and asked me to open it and stick my tongue out.He stuck his cock in my mouth just as he was about to cum and started hurling his healthy sons down my throat.

It started sucking more and less from that day on.I also greatly improved my dick sucking skill, as he had stated.I started stuffing his entire penis into my throat.

One day, while I was at home, he sent me a message instructing me to stop whatever I was doing and immediately visit his house.He appeared eager.So, when I went to his house, I found him covered in sweat and having a big erection.It tasted weird as I went straight to work, so I stopped.He said that he just fucked a girl and couldn't cum because he didn't enjoy it when I asked why.

I was upset because the least he could do was clean his dick, despite the fact that he was cheating.He profusely apologized when he realized how upset I was.He tried to say that he liked girls but only had feelings for me.However, I did not accept his explanation.I stated that I would not tolerate such behavior and put my foot down.

Anyway, I forgave him because I was addicted to his cock, did the right thing regardless, and he blew a huge nut on my face.

He asked me once, as I was mercilessly choking myself with his enormous monster, if I had ever thought about how it would feel if I took him up in my ass hole.My mind was buzzing with all manner of imaginings of what it would be like, despite my stiff fear.

On the same day, while we were on a 69 and I was eagerly sucking his pole, he pointed at me and asked me to sit on his face.I was taken aback once more when I felt a tongue in my booty hole for the very first time.

Sadly, an incident occurred, putting our heavenly session on hold, and Faruq was forced to leave the country. We were both looking forward to me being disvirgined by his torpedo.What took place was that a girl in our neighborhood was well-known among her peers for being generous with her genitals.My brother and his friends have assaulted her on multiple occasions, but she recently became pregnant and stated that she was raped.

This took place in Faruq's house, and he was primarily to blame because he was known for publicly exposing himself.Additionally, this girl's uncle was a high-ranking soldier who was prepared to kill.He was forced to leave the country as things rapidly deteriorated.

Faruq would not be seen by me until many years later.

I suffered greatly from Faruq's absence, and it was not easy to live without him after literally spending more than four years with him every day.

I fell into a deep depression because whenever I thought of us and the wonderful things we did together, I would suddenly feel a lot of sadness and either lose my erection or start to cry.Additionally, a number of thoughts kept coming to mind, particularly the possibility that he was having another person.

I had to force myself to forget him for my own good because everything was wearing me down. To be honest, I had begun to become extremely horny, and wanking was no longer sufficient.Due to the fact that I was unable to experience this with Faruq, I yearned to feel a man's kiss, touch, and most importantly, the sensation of having a man insert his penis into my genital area.

Men in my neighborhood used to give me a lot of compliments all my life, but I never paid any attention to them. As I got older, I started to pay more attention to them.It turned out that many of them liked me, even the so-called "married ones."I could see it in their eyes, so they didn't need to tell me.The only difference between Faruq's and these randy men's looks was that Faruq's was more profound and pure, whereas these men clearly wanted to "peniscise" me. It was similar to how Faruq used to look at me.

I definitely appreciated the attention and desired more, of course.I started using skin care products to make my skin look better and started working out to get in shape.I changed out of my previous dress and put on something more revealing that showed off my toned, glowing skin in no time at all;When I wore thin, loose fabrics that did nothing to conceal my large, soft bum-bum, which wobbled uncontrollably when I walked or went jogging, the compliments from men started pouring in like rain like magic.Funny enough, I didn't get slurs from anyone—I guess it was because I wasn't feminine—but I did get teased for trying to seduce girls—can you imagine how stupid straight people are?

But the women in my neighborhood seemed to be the only ones who were bothered by my pounding body.They would either murmur or look at me with disdain as I passed, as they were unable to speak. I suppose they were smart enough to smell something fishy.

Even Faruq's mother was one of "them"—if only she had known that her only son was the first to inject his sperm into my body.Regarding Faruq's mother, she became a source of contention for everyone.Everyone stopped hearing a word after her son left Nigeria.

She now had the habit of standing on her balcony and speaking loudly while making international calls in an attempt to let the world know that her son was away.

I had wanted to inquire about him several times, but she and her daughters were terrible snubs.

The tension was high at the time, and we avoided Faruq's family like the plague because my brother was involved in the r*pe accusation.

[With regard to the r@pe matter, it was discovered that the perpetrator was a married man who was friends with the girl's family and was working hard to conceal the news.]

Back to my narrative:A man in my neighborhood whom we all referred to as "pastor" was one of my many male admirers.

As kids, my brother and other kids in my neighborhood used to help him run his pharmacy, which was known as a chemist, in the hope that he would give us Vitamin C to lick in return.He has been very fond of me and has often commented on how attractive I am for as long as I can remember.He would jokingly say that he wished I had a sister or that God made me a woman so he could marry me;which will make us both laugh.

Because I was certain that Pastor had a large penis, he was my first target.You see, I had found Faruq changing his clothes in the small room at the back of his shop, where he usually stayed when he couldn't go home, long before I met him.I hurriedly returned to his shop because I had forgotten something while he had sent me on an errand.By doing this, I noticed that the door to the small room was slightly open, and as he was changing clothes, I caught a glimpse of his very long, fat, and limp cock.I didn't pay much attention as I left because I wasn't aware at the time of how much I wanted to please a man's penis.

My initial action was to properly excite his affection for me.I started spending time in his shop, staring intently into his eyes and smiling as we talked.

During one of my visits, I wore a top that was very sheer and did nothing to hide my big, juicy nipples and bulging triceps.He said he had been wanting to ask me why my nipples were so large, like those of a woman, and I told him it was natural. He noticed them right away.

I started gently stroking each of his nipples as we talked because I could tell he was intrigued by the way his eyes kept going to them.He inquired as to why I was touching them after noticing what I was doing.

He choked on his laugh and said, "That means I'd probably faint if someone put their mouth on it," when I said it felt sweet because they were very sensitive.He was making me feel so horny, so I told him to stop, but he kept making me laugh.
He tried to look away but couldn't stop touching my nipples while he was still doing so.As he asked me to stop or go look for a girl, he sucked hard several times.
"What took place with your mouth?" He laughed and said he wasn't a woman when I asked casually.He agreed with me when I said that it was awkward for a woman to suck on my nipple because of the similarities between our breasts.
"If you want to!" "I fit you , make you suck am!"While boldly gently stroking both nipples, I quickly made a joking comment.
He began to giggle and referred to me as a bad boy.
As I briefly stroked my nipples, I began to quietly moan, and despite his plea for me to stop, I paid him no attention.As I stood up to inform him that I was going into his small room, I purposefully propped myself up by placing my hand on his crotch.He was rigid, exactly as I had anticipated.
He neither pushed me away nor responded.He just sat there, his expression very nervous.
As I waited for him, I took off my shirt and laid down on his bed, still stroking my nipples.He entered the room after a brief pause and I heard the main door of his shop lock nearly ten minutes later.He smiled sheepishly and asked me what I wanted, his dick clearly throbbing and rock hard in his pants.
I pulled him closer to me because I wasn't one to talk too much, and we began to frantically kiss.Pastor, who was married and had children, appeared to be gay and starving, just like I was. I started sucking on his thick, long, curved, rock-hard left penis out of genuine desperation, and he loved it.
As his fingers forced their way into my trouser and then into my ass hole, he went mad on my nipples, sucking them dry.He was so rough, and his thick fingers hurt because of it.However, despite my pleas for him to slow down, he was unable to stop.
Surprisingly, my virgin hole accepted as much as two of his fingers despite the fact that I was in pain.I couldn't help but beg him to fuck me as he was intensely kissing and finger-fucking me at the same time.
He came up on top of me and spread my legs apart before opening his mouth to eat my moist pussy, and I lost it completely.As he did various things to me, I thrashed and groaned.
He eventually entered me with calculated patience after positioning me correctly and thoroughly lubricating us both.
Indeed, getting a cock inside my hole was heaven, as I had imagined.
As I praised the pastor's endurance and moaned in a variety of languages, he pounded me hard.He didn't stop for a second; he continued to smash my walls until he flooded my hole with gallons and gallons of fresh milk and growled and shivered.
I loved it, even though my wound was sore and exhausted!I became a dick addict and began to only want giant dicks and more sex.I went from being a pastor to looking for guys online and other men in my neighborhood.To satisfy my insatiable craving, I even traveled to other states to obtain massive dicks.
Faruq showed up eventually.

He appeared young and had gained weight.I stopped by to say hi, like everyone else.All the feelings I thought I'd buried came flooding back when I saw him again, and it appeared that he felt the same way.He offered his sincere apologies for the prolonged silence and explained that his mother—the sole means by which he could communicate with us in Nigeria—had vehemently rejected his requests for contacts—including mine.Strangely, Faruq did not use social media either.

I instinctively agreed when he told me how much he missed me and that he wanted to continue from where we had stopped.To be honest, even after all these years, I never stopped thinking about him.Like before he left, my feelings for him were still fresh.

He invited me over one afternoon while his mother was out of the house.I douched and got ready after I realized what that meant.

He showed me pictures of his new life when I got to his house and gave me some things he had bought for me.He cuddled me as we talked, and then we started kissing slowly but passionately. I was delighted to receive his enormous sugar stick once more, just as he had done in the past. As he suffocated me with his man meat for a sweet moment before asking me to sit on his face, he kept muttering how much he missed me.My cheeks were parted to assist in an excellent invasion of my privacy as I made his face my throne and his tongue mercilessly licked my man's pussy.

His expression changed unexpectedly as I eventually sat on his dick.However, as I began to ride him expertly, I forgot about it because I was too distracted by how delightfully occupied my hole felt.I put one foot firmly on the bed, placed my palms on his neck, and pulled him hard to meet my vigorous riding at some point.

After a blissful time in paradise, Faruq continued to gasp and scream, and I heard him yell loudly as he sprinkled his seeds all over my body.I could see him looking disappointed as we got dressed after cleaning up.He coldly replied, "nothing," when I inquired about the issue.

I was enraged that night when he messaged me and asked me how many people had fucked me since he left.His response shocked me when I asked him why he asked such a question. He informed me that we did not use lubricant and that my pussy was extremely wide.Actually, the saliva from his rimming was what we had used.

I was extremely ashamed.

Naturally, I reacted defensively and screamed at him before hanging up.He called a few days later to apologize and request a meeting, stating that he had missed me.In a posh hotel this time.

Before lunch, we had multiple flings, and he gave me a lovely treat.He informed me that he wanted us to be in a relationship as we drove home the following morning.I genuinely adore Faruq, but I've been a slut for so long that I have no idea where or how to be committed.

Chapter 3

Road trip scenario

"Joy, please stop talking right now!Who said that sex kills?The old woman snapped, "Abeg
(please)Oga (Mister) Armed Robber, Feel free to do it to all of us, joo."
That was typical Mama Tilly, the grandmother of my neighbor.That outburst was triggered by an
occurrence.However, suffice it to say that this story relies on succinct background information.
Leo is my name, and I'm from the suburbs.It's fun to live in the suburbs.I lived in a three-block
apartment complex in Rosewood, Lagos, a few years ago.Ms. Joy, who was in her early thirties
and working for a telecom company, lived in the first apartment. She was slim, pretty,
easygoing, and generally nice.She did not have a husband and lived with her elderly
grandmother.The latter's poise was comparable to that of the compound's Ye Olde One.We
admired her quirky ways and deferred to her.Lady Helen, a genteel Jehovah's Witness in her
forties, owned Apartment 2. Rumors suggested that she had been engaged for ten years to a
pastor who had not yet decided whether or not to marry her.She had a firm sense of what was
right and wrong.Due to the fact that it was a gated compound, it was relatively private and safe.
Although none of them were aware of my sexual orientation, I was bisexual.Nowadays, it was
common for men to be single at thirty.As a result, I occasionally hosted female guests and
occasionally permitted a male friend to spend the night.Since my neighbors were aware of my
affairs with women, it was not out of place to occasionally have a male visitor who, in their own
opinion, could just be a friend or acquaintance.
I couldn't get back to sleep one cold December night around midnight.I inserted a gay
pornographic film and began cuddling myself.A loud voice shouted, "Open this door at once!"
after a sudden bang on my door.Fearing a catastrophe, I jumped to my feet, grabbed my boxer
shorts, and dashed to the door.I assumed either a fire or an accident had occurred.I was
confronted by three massive men wearing masked masks who were each armed with a Glock
and had a menacing expression on their faces.I was terrified at the sight of the men, the guns,
and the three cowering women.
The strongest and tallest of the three shouted, "Come out here."I did as I was asked.I had a
sudden urge to pee because my knees were weak.
We were all directed to the courtyard's center.We had to kneel down.
We followed through without a hitch.

We will now search your rooms and bodies.However, if you are aware of any valuables, go bring them on your own."You will answer to our gun if you hide anything and we find it ourselves," the man said in a quiet but dangerous tone.I was reminded of Luther Vandross by his voice.

We followed in obedience and left the elderly woman with the three men in their respective rooms.

I brought my prized gold chain, iPhone, brand-new Puma kicks, my Hitachi laptop, the 20,000 naira I had saved up to send to my mother to buy a rice bag for Christmas.Others brought something they thought was worthy.

The men looked at each item carefully, and when they were satisfied, the second man said in a similarly guttural voice:

He said, pointing to Helen's apartment, "Oya, you women, enter this room. We are going to fuck you all."He said to me, "Go inside your own room, and no funny business," and he pointed at me.I will blow your head off if you call or notify anyone, understand?"I nodded.I remained dazed.Everything was surreal.I thought it was just a terrible dream.I got up, but then I heard the pleading voice of Ms. Joy:Sirs, please, I beg of you.You can do anything with me, but please do not touch my grandmother in the name of God.Because she is old, her brittle bones may not be able to handle sexual activity.She might even pass away in the process."Joy, please stop talking right now!Who said that sex kills?The old woman snapped, "Abeg (please)Oga (Mister) Armed Robber, Feel free to do it to all of us, joo."

I was close to laughing out loud.The old woman's boldness and the reference to the "Oga Armed Robber" must have taken their breath away the three armed men's stunned expressions.Ms. Joy looked at her obstinate grandmother as if she had suddenly grown horns as the three men suddenly burst into raucous laughter.

I swallowed my laughter and followed the instructions to my room.When the pack leader barged in, I went to turn off the television because I saw the porn movie still playing.I remained fixed on the spot.He took a single glance at the scene on the television and absorbed the information.A large black man was slamming his enormous cock into a small white man's hole.The way he swiveled his head and intensely observed gave the impression of being somewhat fascinated.But I couldn't look at his face.So, you're a snob, right?Yes, you would like to be fucked in the arse.He asked in a sexy way.No sir.I responded defensively, "I was just curious."Liar.I couldn't put my finger on it, but I felt something different about you.I now understand.

He sat on my bed and shifted his enormous weight.Because he was well covered, I was unable to see his face.

He quickly undid the zipper on his denim pants, and from his briefs came a massive shlong.I had never witnessed a dick of that size before.Although only half erect, it appeared to be massive enough to cause harm.It was fat and long.I took a big inhale.I was asked to come over by him.I approached him slowly and knelt down in front of his black, python-like penis, as if in a trance.It throbbed like an agama lizard, and the veins were clearly visible.

"Take it.I recognize your desire.Even though he was threatening me, his voice was still sweet in my ears. "If you dare bite it, I will blow your head off."

I went to town after wetting my lips.I indulgently licked the purple crown.My body was anticipating something significant, and my tongue was hot.Like I had never done before, I

fellated the organ by wrapping my hand around it like a wrist.He lay and set on his elbows and watch me managing on his dick
"Goodness, that is sweet.My friend, keep going.He moaned, "Aaaargh, don't stop."
I sucked with greater fervor.He was under my control.My enthusiasm was heightened by the thought of having control.As I sucked his, I caressed my now enraged partner.I slowed down as he held on to my head.
He gradually shifted and asked me to join him on the bed by taking off my boxers.Vaseline in a jar caught his eye.He lubricated both my hairy ass and his dick with a substantial amount of the jelly.As if I were offering my ass to the gay gods, I lay on my stomach and lifted it.He experimented with my hole and ensured that it had adequate lubrication.The assault followed.The crown of his dick found and prodded my tight, puckered hole with the precision of a fired missile.It stood firm.He made a small push.My hole continued to resist.Then, with a powerful push, he grabbed me by the waist and held me in place.I noticed stars.I tasted my own blood and bit my lower lip to prevent screaming.Before bursting in and out, he took a moment to unwind.As my body became accustomed to his size, the pain gradually subsided.After that, an alien pleasure spread throughout me.My entire body began to itch.I moved alongside him.We waltzed away like two rutting boars as his thrusts gained momentum.His coarse pubic hair grazed my ass cheeks, which felt ticklish, and his huge balls pounded the delicate area between my ball and hole.
A knock at my door woke us up.
"XY, we're finished.Let's go, na," one of the other two shouted outside.Hold on to me.I will arrive!He retorted.
He started actually coming at that precise moment.Spasms filled his entire body as he gave the final blow.The force of his final release made him shake.My interiors were flooded by his thick, creamy cum with the force of Niagara Falls.My rigid spine was shaken as he kissed the back of my neck.His weight was a lot, and his pubic hair made my cheeks itchy.I could feel my balls dumping their loads onto the bed sheets as the final spout of cum exploded.His now-sensitive dick that was still buried within me took pleasure in the constant contraction of my hole as I reached my peak.
We spent about five minutes supine.He then took off his mask, only showing his lips.He had a neatly trimmed mustache.He kissed me then.hard and long.In return, I responded.Then I felt the twitching of our cocks.
He got up and unzipped his pants.
"I will see you once more.Soon, " he said softly.
He gave me a playful smack and then left.
I had to force him to tell the truth.I overheard him telling his partners outside, "Let's roll."
I made an effort to wear a long robe.His sperm began to seep out of my groin.I went outside and rang the doorbell at Ms. Joy's apartment.I went over to hold her because she was crying.Her grandmother was not visible to me.I was afraid to go there.I had the impression that the elderly lady might have passed away.Leo, she followed them.She sobbed and said, "My grandma followed the bastard."Ah, what took place?"Ms. Helen just walked in, looking dazed.She was screaming at him to give her more after he raped her.I rushed to the bathroom because I was about to vomit.She was sniffling and said, "I was hearing their disgusting sounds."I begged the man to do. Ah, otio o.I informed him that I was having menstrual periods and that I would curse

him for life if he touched me.He trusted me.Ms. Helen said indignantly, "I gave him the five thousand naira I hid under my bed instead."She went after them.Ha!"All I could say was that.The grandmother made her return a few days later.We all forgot about the scandalous incident that night because she was smiling so much.In the meantime, I kept dreaming about that intimidating armed robber.Imagine being held, kissed, and fucked once more by that rebel! I went shopping at Shoprite a few months later.My eyes locked with those of a very handsome stranger who was coming from the opposite direction as I was browsing toiletries on a lonely aisle.He had a washboard stomach, a slim waist, and was tall with broad shoulders.He was sporting a gray tights-style T-shirt that showed off his six packs, chest, and muscular arms.I was reminded of the dreamily sexy Idris Alba by his full lips and chin cleft.As if he controlled the world, he purposely walked.I was awed by his magnetism as his measured steps got closer to me.My lips become dry.I had never experienced anything like that in my life.I felt as though I was with a celestial being.

His snow-white teeth were out of this world, and he smiled and said, "Hello."His voice had a tinge of familiarity about it.I mumbled, "He-hello," sounding like an insane teenager.Please spare a minute, he asked politely.That sound!Sure," I said as I zombie-like followed him.He entered through a door.I did the same.It was a workplace.With a mocking wave of his hand, he said, "My friend is the manager, but she is a lousy decorator," and he laughed softly.I was perplexed and asked, "Excuse me, what am I doing here?"I never did shoplift.He said in a hoarse voice, "Let me show you something."He grabbed me in his arms and pressed his lips firmly to mine before I could say Jack Robinson.We were kissing each other ferociously like sex-starved brutes before I could gather my thoughts.After that, I suddenly woke up.The one was him!Holly and Mollyas I continue to exist!

I stopped engaging and took a breather.After that, I slapped him hard on the left cheek.He didn't even move.What did that serve?He asked quietly, "How daring of you to tell me you would soon return when you never did.You now had the audacity to attack me in a shopping mall!I said it with the same fury and pettiness.I apologize.I felt awful.I'm not a thief.We took actions to raise funds for Dylan.Everyone who we approached for assistance turned their backs on us while he was in the hospital awaiting a kidney transplant.He went on to explain, "We were desperate."I see.So, why was my groin attacked?Why was the grandmother of my friend raped?"We enjoyed having sexual relations with each other.Haassan was actually raped by your friend's grandmother.The first time he had sex with the ruddy old crone opened a new chapter in his life for him.He still fantasizes about her every day," he chuckled.She is not that.I conceded, reluctantly, "She missed it, and I think it made her less grumpy."

After that, a thought came to me.What about the weapons?

They didn't exist.He gave a big grin and said, "We got them from the Community Playhouse's costume room."I remarked indignantly, "You certainly had us on a dime."So, am I redeemed?I am wearing your gold chain in memory of my first gay sex, which turned out to be the best I have ever had, and I have your iPhone still secured.I suddenly became hot.I went to him this time and started the kiss.We were so absorbed in it that we didn't hear anyone enter.An amused woman said, "Hey guys, get a room."I assumed she was the supervisor.a seemingly permissive one.Dear Sylvia,Then we both realized that we hadn't introduced ourselves. This is—

We gave each other the sheepish look from Tom and Jerry comics as we looked at each other.

Chapter 4

Brotherhood secret

I have four brothers, and three of my male cousins stayed with us as well.Despite the fact that my brothers and cousins were all men, we appeared to share a similar physical appearance, which contributed to our street popularity.Guys wanted to hang out with us, and girls wanted to date us.

The "brother" Onochie who is the subject of this narrative was the eldest of my brothers and cousins.He was given control of the house by my parents, and they made sure that we all respected him to the fullest, which is why he was called "brother."

We didn't like him because he was annoyingly direct and didn't cut corners. Maybe that's why my parents treated him like royalty because he was their eyes and ears when they were away. Despite how much we didn't like him, no one could deny that Onochie was a fucking hunk.He was built tall and had a big, fat dick.How was I aware?because when my parents weren't home, we usually walked around the house in boxers or naked.His package was full to the brim.In point of fact, he was my first crush and the first indication that I liked men.

Additionally, Onochie presented a very religious persona to the women who desired him, which was a huge disappointment.

After our morning prayers one day, my dad told us that his friend's son from the UK would be coming in a few days and would be staying with us until he found a place of his own.He advised us to greet him rather than "corrupt him."

Since the visitor didn't share his room, my mother suggested that he stay in oneochie's room. Brother Onochie clearly did not like the idea, but he had no choice.

The day of the visitors' arrival is quickly approaching.

I had just returned from my mother's shop, where I typically assisted her with sales.When I entered the living room, my dad was sitting next to this extraordinarily athletic man.I literally had no words.As I gave him a very gentle handshake, all I did was smile like a goat.

After a formal introduction by my dad, I learned his name, Russell.

Russell and Onochie became very close over time, to the point where they wore each other's clothes and were always with each other.

I got envious of this.

Except for me, it was viewed as a friendship-based brotherhood by everyone.But everything in me yelled "GAY" from the core.

I had forgotten one night that I hadn't given Onochie the money from the shop's daily sales, which were supposed to be deposited in the bank the next day.Even though it was nearly midnight and everyone was asleep, I had to give the money to Onochie because if I didn't, he would most likely tell my mother, who would kill me.

I dragged myself to his room, exhausted.Because it was past midnight and everyone had gone to bed, the house was quiet.When I got to the door to Onochie's room, I could hear soft music coming from behind the door, but then I swear I could also hear moans.My suspicion was confirmed when I pressed my ears against the door.Indeed, something was taking place behind the door.

As I vigorously knocked on the door, my face turned green with envy.

"Who is that?"

A worried voice asked.

The voice immediately sounded like Onochie's.

There was a long silence when I called my name.

"yes?"

He asked inane questions.

It was clear that I had interrupted his show.

I informed him that I needed to hand over the shop returns.

"Move on."He directed.

From inside, I could hear scurrying, and then the door unbolted in a few seconds.

Onochie approached the door.

You know that fake look that someone gives when they say they just woke up from a long nap?Exactly!!!!Onochie exuded authority.

He kept pretending to rub his eyes.My instinct told me that he was either naked or hiding his erection behind the door because he stood behind it so that it wouldn't open fully.

I could make out what appeared to be Russell adjusting himself beneath the sheets, even though the room was dark.

I said, "Hello Russell, I didn't know you were awake;"as I entered the room, I tried to be friendly;pushing the door back a little and brushing aside Onochie's solid, hairy body.

Onochie switched on the light and inquired as to why I was disrupting his sleep.He was obviously furious.I casually informed him that I had arrived to deliver the sales proceeds.

As I handed him the cash, he extended his hands.Even though his pantsuit still gave the impression of a demon, his dick was now partially erect.I could clearly see the entire dick and the black bush of his pubic hair because he was not wearing underwear.

The smell of testosterone filled the room.With the look Onochie was giving me, I would have died instantly if looks could kill.

I casually greeted Russell as I turned to him, and as I was about to inquire about his day, he asked, "Please, can we do this some other time?"I need some rest after such a busy day, so it's late.He responded politely but dismissively, "Thank you."

Wow!!!!Did he just criticize me?

I was shattered.in a literal sense.I simply gave a head nod and left the room feeling defeated.

Russell weighed heavily on my mind for the next few days.I couldn't get rid of him, but it was obvious that he loved his cousin and not me.

When I got home from the shop one day, the atmosphere was just "wrong."

Russell has been robbed and beaten, and he is currently in the hospital.When I inquired about the issue, my mother informed me.

My instinct told me right away that it was a lie.Given that Onochie and she are always together, where was she when this occurred?I inquired, but no one responded.

Russell went home that evening to get some of his belongings.He insisted that he spend the night in a hotel, despite my parents' repeated pleas for him to do so. He appeared to have been severely beaten.At the time, Onochie wasn't home.

When Onochie returned, he had a very different account of the location where Russell claimed his assault occurred.His own version of the story seemed completely bizarre to me, but I suppose everyone thought of him as a saint who had no faults and could not be questioned.

Russell disappeared from my family over time and never returned with the rest of his belongings.On the other hand, it appeared as though Onochie was going down a dark hole.He began to lose weight, became extremely touchy, and became easily and unnecessarily enraged.

When the power went out one night, my brothers, cousins, and I went outside to get some fresh air.I entered the house because I felt the need to use the bathroom.I finished and was about to go outside to see my parents when I heard a voice from the kitchen.It was, in my mind, Onochie's voice.I wouldn't have bothered, but the word "Russy," which is Russell's nickname, and the voice, which sounded like a guy talking to his girlfriend, caught my attention.

In order to hear more, my naturally "busy body" self began to quietly move closer to the kitchen.Whoever was on the phone, Onochie was begging.

I could barely make out the recipient's voice in the stillness of the night.

"However, you were the cause of it; why did you collect his number?"You even showed no respect for the fact that....so?Yes, you initiated me.Onochie's voice began to rise with bitter venom as you initiated me.

"yes!!!I entered your mouth after you bitched your way through my cock.My sperm was swallowed by you, and I fucked your arse.It appeared from his voice that he intended to humiliate his caller with such remarks.

Hearing this made me want to faint.Of all people, Onochie.

"Is it because I didn't want you to fuck my arse??? You're dreaming," she said.

He hissed, "you too- fuck off." He must have hung up because the entire house fell into a grave silence.I quickly ducked as his footsteps approached.

I was both so happy and so sorry for him.My uptight cousin has tasted the "no going back fruit," making me happy, and, most importantly, my adorable Russell sucks and swallows.

I had an instant erection when I imagined Onochie's big dick entering and exiting Russel's mouth and butt.

I met Russell by accident in a gas station a few months later.Excitedly, we hugged and said hello.I had assumed he had returned to the UK and was surprised to see him.We exchanged numbers and I went to visit him now that he had a job and lived in Lagos.

In Victoria Island, he owned a stunning apartment with two bedrooms.Indeed, Russell was thriving for himself.

I started going to see him a lot, and on one of my visits, I told him about my feelings for him and that I knew about his affair with Onochie.

Russell's demeanor changed when he heard ONOCHIE'S name.He sat in silence and said nothing.He refused to discuss the incident that occurred between them.
Despite my empathy for his feelings and knowledge of his sadness, my horny hormones prevented me from doing so.I got up from where I was sitting, walked up to him, and started touching him without thinking about it.He tried to stop me, but he couldn't stop me.
He eventually allowed me to have my way after a lot of pressure.Russell sat motionless and stared at me when I took off his shorts.I held his semi-erect dick, which was so warm in my hands.Are you aware of your actions?He pressed.
I did not bother to respond.All I did was start sucking him by placing my mouth over his dick.He made an effort to move my head away, but I was resolute, so he left me.After repeatedly sucking on him, I quickly changed into my clothes.
I took off his shirt and caressed his naked body as I was mesmerized by his muscled body, even though he seemed uninterested in the whole thing.I tried kissing him, but he refused. I licked his nipples.I started grinding my cock on his by laying my now-naked body on top of him. As I attempted to insert his dick into my ass hole, he remained motionless.I hadn't reached my lowest point in my life at the time, so His dick couldn't penetrate me despite being average.Therefore, I resolved to simultaneously suck and wank him until he entered my mouth. At the time, I had never taken cum in, so I forcefully swallowed it to avoid offending him.

Russell did not move from his position.He merely sat down and appeared miserable.As I said my goodbyes, I stayed at the spot and pecked him.
Russell made me literally obsessed.Every day, I texted and called him.I began using my pocket money to buy him presents.In fact, I began stealing money from my mother's shop in an effort to curry favor with him, but he remained uninterested.
Russell sent me a text asking me not to visit his house anymore and not to tell anyone what had happened between us.Despite his verbal and physical abuse of Onochie, I knew it was because he still had feelings for him.He continued to adhere to his decision despite my pleadings.
I was obviously heartbroken, but as time passed, I forgot about Russell, met a wonderful man who is now my boyfriend, and started dating him.
I didn't go to my hometown with my parents during the holiday season because I had an important exam early next year.Additionally, I had promised to attend the 60th birthday celebration of my boyfriend's father.
Brother Onochie was home as well.He hasn't traveled with our family during the holidays since I can remember.He usually stays behind to look after the house and shops.
I neglected to mention that Onochie had changed around that time.He wasn't as rigid and irritating as he had been in the past.He understood what I had kind of said to him without me saying it out loud.We got along after I introduced him to my boyfriend, whom he refers to as my "half."Also, I kind of knew that he was back with Russell, but because we were so different in age, we never talked about his love life.
When he was on the phone or on video call with Russell, who was away in the UK at the time, I frequently witnessed him having a massive erection that he was no longer ashamed to hide when I was present.

I once intended to sleep at my boyfriend's house;However, I made the decision to return home around 1 a.m. because of the mishap.I saw Russell's car parked inside the compound as I returned home.He appeared to have returned from the UK.

I thought to myself, "Onochie must be absolutely thrilled."I was certain that the house's complete silence was not an indication that it was empty as I entered through the back door.

I simply made my way through the darkness to Onochie's room without turning on the light. I could hear Toni Braxton, his favorite artist, singing from behind his slightly opened door.There were lights on.The sight I saw when I gently opened the door could best be described as divine. Both men were fast asleep and naked.It was adorable to see Onochie hold Russell in such a protective manner.On the other hand, Onochie's enormous but still moist dick almost made me faint.Their jaw, beard, and cheeks were covered in dried sperm;Perhaps they were kissing each other with cum in their mouths.Enoch's stomach had a lot of dried cumin.They clearly sucked until they fell asleep.

I sent a picture of the two men asleep to my boyfriend, who had doubts about my sexuality and Onochies Godzilla dick.Fortunately, he wasn't sleeping at that late hour because he saw it and responded right away, effectively ending our disagreement.We laughed about it, and when Bae said that he was horny because he had seen the picture, I suggested something strange, and he agreed.

After the call, Bae came over, and we stayed up in the living room watching movies and fucking.We went to bed naked because we knew Onochie would feed his eyes when he woke up because his room led directly to the sitting room.

Onochie came down and saw us, as I predicted.Because I was a light sleeper, I heard him come down and winked at him when our eyes met.Russell popped up all of a sudden as he reciprocated my smile.

He cooed, "ohhh kayyy."

I started kissing my boyfriend as he lazily stood up.My fingers found his still-moist hole as I slid my hands down his smooth back.He let out a soft moan and began to whine about his waist as I stuck my finger into his honey-saturated love tunnel.My gaze caught Onochie as my boo rubbed his finger on mine.As he observed us, his dick stood horribly erect.

Russell began stuffing his mouth with hard igbo meat as he sank to his knees.

I was drenched in water and mounted after my boyfriend spit on his hands.The manner in which my man rides is one thing that drives me crazy.I was pleased that he was not afraid to demonstrate how well he pleases me, and he truly knows his duty.

They observed my boo bounce on me like an Indian rubber ball while Russell was seriously sucking on Onochies pipe.

I heard Onochie tell Russell that he wanted to urinate, but Russell seemed to ignore him.They were having a playful argument about something I couldn't understand, I could hear.My lover and I were both really shocked by the next thing.

Russell was opening his mouth as Onochie was urinating.My man and I watched in complete astonishment.

I suddenly felt like my bladder was full, but I'm not sure if it was a reflex.Because I wanted to pee, I asked my boyfriend to excuse me.He excused himself and led me to the toilet and bathroom for guests.He asked me if I had ever considered urinating inside him as I was about to do so.Although it was coming from him, it opened my mind to new concepts, so I was somewhat surprised.He said yes when I asked him if he would like to try it.

I began loading my first sips of the day by inserting my still hard prick into his juicy cunt while bending over.It's better to feel than to hear the sensation of having your prick drown inside a flooded hole that happily grips your shaft.

From the living room, I could hear screams and yelling.My boy friend and I hurriedly joined the fun.

With his head buried in a throw pillow, Russell was hunched over on the sofa.As Onochie's ridiculous prick hurriedly slammed into him, he was moaning uncontrollably.

Alongside Russell, my boyfriend positioned himself on the sofa.However, in contrast to Russell, he was lying on his back on the sofa and raising his legs in the air, revealing the open, juicy hole that was still leaking with urine.

I positioned myself and once more entered his treasure cave.

The sight of my dick appearing and disappearing into my man's ass while he moaned while I;On the other hand, she was mesmerized by Russell's wildly stretched ass on Onochi's yam tuber.

I honestly have no idea how it happened, but I suddenly noticed that I was sucking and licking Onochie's right nipples while his sausage-like fingers finger-fucked my ass.I was forced to scream out of sweet pain as he pushed his fingers so deeply into my hole.

I saw Russell and my boyfriend jacking off each other's dick as they moaned in ecstasy while I was jolting and screaming from being fingered.We swooped as if we were in each other's heads.

I felt like I was entering an abyss as I entered Russell.My dick couldn't fit through his wide hole.I glanced at Onochie as he attempted to enter my boyfriend's room, but from their expressions, it appeared that they found it unsatisfactory.We therefore swooped once more.

Onochie urged me to "suck my breast" (breast), and I resumed my duties.The assault continued as soon as his thick fingers found my ass hole.

I felt my balls expand quickly, and I started pouring thick, creamy juice into my guy's hole.Onochie started to scream, "Russyyyy.....its coming....Russyyy.....it's coming..." as if we were all wired. With the speed of light, Russell opened his mouth and caught every drop of sperm shooting from Onochie's Jericho penis as he frantically wanked his cock, which was also releasing creamy white bullets.During the same time, my boyfriend also began to cum.

We have a rule in my relationship that says we won't waste sperm;so promptly as my man was cumming, I'd put my mouth over his chicken and was taking his nutrients and minerals to feed and recharge my body similarly as I have;his.

As Russell's sperm dripped down their jaws and beards, Onochie and Russell were locked in a passionate kiss.

We were all worn out.Our boyfriends prepared us breakfast after our shower, and we went out later that day.

I'm glad a member of my family plays for my team.

Chapter 5

THE CHALLENGE

I was caught sexing in an unfinished building my first year at the university.
I had been chatting with a particular person online for some time, and he was traveling through the state where I taught.He listened to my pleas and stopped by.Sadly, my covert girlfriend, however, refused to leave and appeared out of nowhere like a ghost.
Because we were both so horny, my guest and I had to find another option.He wanted to stay in a hotel, but since I needed the money and he didn't have much, I suggested we go with an unfinished building.
I insisted, and he vehemently rejected it.Additionally, the majority of the students had left for home, so the atmosphere was friendly.
We found a safe spot among the rooms in the unfinished building and got to work after he finally agreed.I touched my toes for him to fuck the crap out of my man hole with his big juicy dick after I had satisfied myself by sucking him.
A few minutes into his ferocious pounding, one person whistled in disbelief, and another shouted,See "homo."It was a miracle that I didn't pass out right away.We would have quickly disengaged and pretended as if nothing had happened if we hadn't heard a single sound of someone approaching.However, we were completely caught with red hands!
As I bent down, I recognized the men whose penis was still in my hole.One of them, a man we students referred to as "double cross," belonged to the community vigilantes.Even school cultists feared and dared him not because he was their leader and was so brutal.
I had previously met him one-on-one over an allegation prior to that incident.In my hostel, a guy had accused his roommate of trying to rape him. It was a funny and messy story.The individual claimed that his roommate placed a charm on his penis in order for it to hold, and then he instructed him to enter his ass hole.He claimed that the charm was broken because he seriously prayed, but he had already released sperm into his roommate's hole.You can visualize the absurdity).
What role did I play?My friend is his roommate.

I was aware that both men had sex multiple times, which is the truth.I had been told by his roommate's friend that whenever they sex, the guy would start asking God for forgiveness, even if he started the sex.My friend stopped responding to his nighttime advances because perhaps he became fed up with his drama.

When double cross asked, I denied not being gay to save my neck.However, I was asked to purchase drinks for the vigilantes even at that point.Fortunately, the stupid person who accused my friend suddenly lost his mind when asked, "How he could allow another man to rub charm on his penis and fuck him to the point of ejaculation without raising alarm or fighting him off in the process?" My friend was cleared of the charges.

The case came to an end when he was eventually asked to pay a fine.

I was there now.Using a man's penis that was buried deep within my anus to touch my toes.What was my justification?

I was immediately recognized by Double Cross.He told his men to stop beating us because they wanted to.He ordered us to keep fucking so he could watch and pulled out a cheap local pistol.His men, clearly irritated at seeing men fuck, were perplexed by his interest and consent, but they were unable to question him.

He insisted that we stay until my guest left (ejaculated).In point of fact, he instructed us to act as though he and his men weren't watching us.They started smoking marijuana and told my guest to start fucking me harder.Double Cross asked my guest to show him how big he was at some point by showing him his penis.Double cross blew a loud whistle and said that women should fear me when he did that.He made me yell loudly and stop acting like I wasn't enjoying it after I was reintroduced.And I did as instructed.

My guest miraculously left, and they checked my groin to make sure.

They gave my guest until the octave of five to leave the building, and he sprinted out of there without a second's hesitation after collecting all of the physical cash he had on him.They hit him on the back of the head as he ran away.

Regarding me, I was instructed to visit their office the following day at the same time in order for them to "treat my matter."

I was in complete panic as I got home.Like many wives, my girlfriend was still there—a pillar of salt.I immediately ended the relationship and yelled at her to GET OUT!!!!! when she started asking me silly questions about where I went.Nagging was the last thing I wanted when I was in complete fear.

I went to their so-called office the following day.It wasn't even an office; rather, it was more like a home with a variety of shady, scary-looking criminals dressed as vigilantes.

When a voice yelled, "homo boy," I had just crossed the gate.It was double dealing.I nearly passed out, but I kept my composure.During my visit, nothing transpired.I was told to "feel at home," as opposed to being beaten up as I had anticipated.

I ordered food and alcoholic beverages for him and his boys from a nearby restaurant.That day, I spent close to N20,000.Double Cross began openly asking me very embarrassing questions about my sexuality while I was there.He requested that I attend the following days, as well as the following ones.I started coming to his house on a regular basis because of that.

In school, double cross became my shield.He was there whenever something happened.He dealt with kito situations effectively even when my friends faced them.I and my friends were safe from cultists at my school.

Did I also mention that Double Cross took me to a whorehouse to see if I could fist-fight with a prostitute?It was a complete failure.I threw up and struggled to get an erection.He cracked up at me throughout.Additionally, he had previously requested that I call my guest so that he could watch us fuck again, but the man had, regrettably, blocked me on every platform on the very same day at the unfinished building.

Double cross was a peculiar anomaly.He frequently stated to me that he desired to observe how my groin received larger men once more.He appeared to have developed a gay vouyer fetish as a result of that incident.However, for no apparent reason, it never took place.

After graduating, I served in the military, moved to another state, and got a job.

Life went on, and I didn't hear from the double cross for more than five years until the day he called me out of the blue.

He had gotten my number after meeting one of my university friends.He informed me that he was getting married for the second time and that he wanted me to help out as a groomsman.He was ecstatic when I sent him a generous amount of cash.

He started asking me one day while we were talking on the phone if I still took dicks in my ass hole.It sounded like there was already a fight because I could hear a voice in the background. He explained to me, "My friend was arguing with me that no ass hole could comfortably take it because women run away and complain about his dick size."He started exaggerating to his friend the size of the dick I had taken at the unfinished building years ago as they argued.His friend did not have faith in him and insisted that he was lying.

Double Cross wanted to bet, but his friend refused because I was a guy and he wasn't homo.However, Double Cross would not be amused.He said that the deal was "if i could take dick (or not)" rather than "if i was a guy or not." He also said that his friend was a coward.

The argument went on for a long time, and it seemed like his friend was getting the message.He called me back on video after he double-crossed and asked to see my photos.I saw a large, old man who looked very ugly and rough.

He said, "Na clean guy o," as he looked at me.

He inquired about my name and advised me not to be offended by his friend's trick.But I told him straight up that he would lose the bet if he doubled down.He was clearly challenged.

"E act like you want to die."As he tried to shield his pride and ego, he spoke in defense.The Double Cross, his friend, was making things worse.He clearly became enraged as he continued to make fun of him.

He warned, "I will tear your nyash o."

But I called him bluff and double-crossed him. He promised that if he touches me, I would run away.He was not ready to hear Double Cross.He insisted that it was actually him and his friend;who will contest?

Evidently, this was a "dare" situation.

I traveled to Asaba two days prior to the wedding and stayed in the hotel that also served as the venue for the wedding reception.

Three men who appeared suspicious showed up in my room with double cross.As they all drank and smoked, they openly discussed their "operations."When I inquired about his big-dick friend, he informed me that he was on his way.

He answered the phone and gave the person my room number a few seconds later.

"He is here."

He turned to his friends and told them that he wanted to talk to me alone about something.A very tall, bulky man was already at the door, dressed in baggy jeans, a large jersey, big white snickers, and a baseball cap that pulled all the way down to his nose, looking like a 90s hip hop rap artist.He received a strange language code and a handshake from the men leaving.It was evident that they "belonged" to the same "brotherhood."

"Boy!!!!...."The visitor spoke to me in a rough voice that made it sound like gravel was stuck in his throat.The curious man on the phone with the alleged "big dick" was immediately the one whose voice I recognized.

In person, he appeared much older than on the video call.

"So, wouldn't you be the one who collects women's penises?"As he stared at me as though I had no idea what I was up against, he asked, his voice heavy with arrogance.As he smoked, he started rolling a blunt and sprinkled something on it, creating an unpleasant odor.When he gave me his blunt, I took a few puffs and thought, "GOSH!"My brain felt like it had exploded with church bells.As I struggled to control the high, both men laughed at me as the room literally danced.

His friend responded when Double Cross said something that sounded like their fraternal language.After doing this a few times, the double cross said, "Carry on."

His friend started taking off his clothes, which surprised me.I also observed a wound that appeared to have been caused by a bullet, despite the fact that his black, shiny body was covered in scars.His very long, flaccid penis was revealed when he pulled down his shorts.

"You don't fear, do you?"He said it with menace.

On the other hand, Double Cross was clearly excited.He asked me to get an erection from his friends' penis.At first, I was shy and hesitant, but it appeared that neither man was patient at all. I observed how, even in a soft state, the numerous network of veins traveled throughout the penis artificially while holding the very fat dick in my hand.I began to slowly kiss his solid, thick body as I rubbed it.Because I was worshiping this man as I would, it might have been what they gave me to smoke;my partner.

He moaned, "fuck," as my tongue found his tiny nipples.

I feathered caressed his ribs while mouth-pleasing his manly nipples, making him stiffen to my touch.It had already grown in size and length by the time my hand got to his penis.He was a 12 in every way.

FACT!!!!!

He was a big man!

He was a huge man!

I took my lubricant out of my bag and led him to the edge of the bed.I started working my hole with my lubricated fingers as I knelt on the bed and stuffed my face with his enormous man meat.Before turning around so that he could enter my newly opened hole, I made sure that I could comfortably insert four fingers into it.

Sadly, the penetration was not as simple as I had anticipated.His friend slammed me hard, and it hurt like hell!!!!!!Only bottoms will comprehend the agonizing pain this could cause.

To keep me quiet, Double Cross had to quickly close his mouth.

As my rectum was brutally stabbed, I felt my hole pulled and grow so large.I've never been fucked like that in my entire life.His huge balls were smashing into my own balls as he fucked my hole, which was really painful.Double Cross, whose hand was still in my mouth, was whispering, "Take it...yes take it," into my ears as my body shivered in agony.He comfortingly patted my head with the other hand.

He slapped away my hand and intensified his thrust as I reached behind him to urge his friend to slow down.

Even though I no longer had an erection, cum continued to pour out of my dick hole.

I was flipped over on my back and re-penetrated almost immediately with a single powerful move.

I was no longer speaking to Double Cross.His friend was, in contrast.As he gripped me tightly from beneath my back with his other hand over my mouth, his entire body weight was on me.

The noise coming from my ass hole became so loud as he pounded on me that it sounded like a bucket of water was empty inside.I could hear another voice moaning in the background with a rapid slurping sound, as if someone were wanking, despite his groaning.

I could tell it was a double-cross.But I couldn't turn my head to see what his friend was doing because his friend was holding my mouth tightly.

As his friend fucked my brains out, it seemed like he was frantically masturbating.I began to feel myself approaching climax as my dick was crushed between our stomachs and his movement was causing friction.Double Cross, who was also grunting and moaning like an animal, was clearly cumming, and I was certain of that.

As it spread throughout our stomachs, my dick found that he could no longer bear the sensation.He paused for a few seconds and began to growl very loudly as I struggled to contain my elation.Inside my hole, I could feel several squirts.His hands suddenly left my mouth, and we began passionately kissing.He fucked me very slowly, as if he was enjoying the sweet wetness of my hole, and we sucked each other's tongues and lips.

He puffed as he stood up and went to the bathroom, "You try...you too much."

As he praised his friend in languages I didn't understand, Double Cross was exuberant and happy.As I lay down on the bed, he even began to spray me with cash.

I was unable to stand for more than 30 minutes.His friend said, "you get sweet toto shaa." as he grabbed my soft ass hard and put his fingers inside after I managed to get up.

He asked, "you enjoy am?" in a husky, etotic whisper.

I replied, "Yeah."

"Hmmmmm??? ...You mean "weed?"As he got very close to me, he gave me a big kiss and whispered to me. He also wriggled his finger in my ass and made very watery sounds as he did so.

Double Cross asked his friend how he could stay so long during sex, and he said that he did two rounds, the second of which took longer.

It was no wonder that my hole was so soaked.

He told Double Cross, who couldn't stop talking about how much of a "bad ass fucker" his friend was, "This guy nyash too sweet no be small."

Funny thing is that they didn't talk about the bet when they left.The money that was thrown at me was N35,000. I counted it.I had a lot of pain the following day.I was told by Double Cross that he had given my number to his friend because he had asked for it.

I got a call from his friend informing me that he had my number.Our conversation was brief; I guess he doesn't talk much.

I found out on the wedding day that he was the best man.Because they all adhered to a specific color code, ninety percent of the men in attendance were members of their fraternity.Double crossing probably occupied the highest position.
He boldly approached me during the reception and instructed us to go to my suit.
He said firmly, "I want to feel you."
My body began to get very hot on its own.I no longer felt the pain in my hole.I didn't hesitate at all.I went with him.I turned around as I left the hallway to see double cross nodding and giving me a thumbs up.
We did not take off our clothes when we got to my room.We just fucked and took off our pants.He entered me without my hole struggling, which surprised me.It opened effortlessly.Even though it was brief, the sex was so sweet.It must have been because my man's pussy was still recovering from the most recent severe beating.
We kissed passionately after we both blew out our cum.After he asked me to briefly suck his nipples, we pulled up our pants and went down to join the wedding guests.

Chapter 6

FOR THE LOVE OF WEED

I have never been comfortable playing the bottom half in sex.Even though I imagine how it would feel to have a cock plow me and fantasize about getting fucked, I never even tried to put my finger in my butthole.This is because I have always believed that once someone starts acting on their thoughts, they will eventually form a habit that will be difficult to break.Additionally, I must confess that the bottom-shaming among community members played a significant role.I detested the label "sister."

Being a weed smoker, I was among the first to look for a "corner" or joint where I could meet other smokers and smoke when my family moved to another part of Lagos.

It took me a few days to find the hideout, which was well hidden from view by a brook (stream). I didn't find it difficult to blend in with the guys, even though, as is typical of any weed joint, there were a lot of guys whose identities were a mystery.I knew I was safe as long as I didn't bring them home or do anything illegal. We were like family by weed.

Kufre is the name of a man who lives on my street.He (kufre) rode a commercial tricycle known as keke-napep along our street, and his mother owned a business nearby.

Kufre was a bad boy with a lot of bad boy swag to match.Even though we did see each other while he was working as a road transporter, we never got a chance to talk until the day I met him in a smoker's joint.

Once weed is involved, it's very easy to "flow" and get along with anyone, as every weed smoker knows.Everyone is treated like family at the joint.We talked about personal matters without being judgmental, gave each other advice, and shared everything, from food to marijuana.

So, one day at the joint, we were talking about how often we did or should do masturbation and how often.The conversation was very open and honest.Kufre stated that he only drinks on weekends after everyone had offered their opinion.When I inquired as to why, he stated that weekends were his days off from work.

One of the guys started making fun of Kufre's dick, saying that it should be part of a community.I inquired about the man's knowledge of that, and he replied that he had previously caught Kufre wanking, which we all laughed about.He continued by stating that he was skeptical that any prostitute would take his cock;and that was the beginning of our collective discussion of them (prostitutes).

Except for Kufre and me, of course, all the guys present acknowledged that they patronize them.In fact, Kufre strongly opposed the concept of sex pay.He says that because he worked hard to earn his money, his money is important to him. As a result, he would rather wank and get what he wants than pay for it.

Even though I don't like Dicks, I suddenly found myself thinking about everything.I was fixated on his cock throughout the discussion, and he noticed I was looking, but somehow he didn't seem to care.

I took advantage of the opportunity to talk to him, and that's how we got to know each other and became good friends.He would either greet me briefly or honk the horn of his tricycle whenever he drove by my house.Funny thing is that my parents liked him and welcomed him because we always bought our goods from his mother's shop (where he also delivers them to our doors).

I also have to admit that ever since we talked about wanking at the joint that day, my crush on Kufre has increased by a whopping threefold to the point where I started imagining having him fuck me with his monster cock.I started using my finger on myself for the very first time in my life.

I needed to smoke one chilly Friday evening, so I went to the joint.I was surprised to find that it was isolated when I got there.There was not a soul to be seen.I assumed it was because of the afternoon's torrential downpour.I saw Kufre riding his tricycle as I was getting ready to leave.I could tell that he was also curious about where everyone was.

We welcomed;He also shared my belief that the devastation was caused by the torrential downpour.

I was hoping to purchase a blunt on-site, but I didn't have one.He;on the other hand, hoped to locate a seller and had just enough for one.I was relieved that he was willing to share his marijuana, even though it appeared that we were both at a loss.

I waited while he cleaned his tricycle;He wrapped his blunt after finishing.The sun had already vanished, and it was getting close to dark.Already, crickets were chirping, and the mood was so laid-back.While Kufre, who had finished wrapping the blunt and lighting it, stood almost above me, I had sat under a mango tree.I could clearly see the outline of his penis on his shorts because he was so close.He was obviously not wearing underwear.

After taking a few puffs, he passed the blunt.Despite the fact that the Ritzier's spit was wet, I took a few drags and passed it on.It was a substantial blunt, just enough to elevate us both sufficiently.I casually inquired of him as we smoked, considering that it was Friday.

He replied, "sure thing."

The silence was strange.

"Is your prick big true?"I inquired

He replied, "e try."

I said, "I for like see am oh," expecting him to correct me.He said, "unto say you want confirm?" with a chuckle.

I responded, "Yes, yes."

He chuckled once more, and to my surprise, he pulled a long, limp, fat prick out of the corner of his shorts.

"Shit!!!"As I impulsively reached for his dick, I gasped.As he pulled the corner of his shorts down, he gave a slight jerk away and started laughing.

I begged, "abeg show me again."

He resisted and pulled his shorts down to the waist, exposing the entire length and thick bush.

"Oh boy, I see a prick!"As I reached for it, I groaned.As I held his monster in my hand in utter awe, he didn't jerk away this time. Instead, he just smiled and smoked with pride.
I continued, still amazed, "and the tin never stand o."
He agreed, "I tell you o...the tin never stand."
As his soft meat began to stiffen on my hand as I began to gently stroke his cock, he began to chuckle and retreated from me.
"Guy, what are you doing? Which level?"He pressed.
I replied, "Relax.. I just want to see how you will be when you rise."
He continued, "But bros e get as e be nah," asking, "Why do you dey shame like say you be woman?"I questioned him in a way.
I continued with a little bit of hardness in my voice:I don't think I'm a man like you.Mhen, unwind, abeg.When he handed the blunt to me, all he said was "Abi......"As I smoked the blunt, I reached for his cock.It began to thicken gradually as I slowly stroked it.It was an absolutely perfect monster cock.I took a whiff of marijuana and gently blew the smoke along the thick cock of his.
He cooed, "na so..."I gave him the blunt, which was now covered in our saliva, after taking another puff.I simultaneously exhaled smoke from my mouth and wrapped my mouth around his wonderful prick as he took a whiff.
"What are they doing, do you not?"He asked, gasping incoherently.
Even though I'm tall, I've perfected the art of oral sex, whether through blowjobs or rimming.I was very proud of it because it was my signature of providing my partner with maximum satisfaction.He rocked his waist even further into my mouth as I sucked down on Kufre's pole of disaster.
"What are you doing, nahhhh, guy?"his weird falsetto voice as his hips slightly arched forward once more, pushing his swollen pole deeper into my oral tunnel).
As I continued to mouth-fuck his pole, I ignored him.

.

I suddenly accelerated my bj speed as he grabbed my head, stood at ease for balance, and began assaulting my throat with his big fuck pole. I don't know if it was the weed, the blow job, or both that seemed to let us loose control.I couldn't care less if I could breathe because I was so high.
He violently began to fuck scatter my throat after pressing my head all the way down his pole and holding it in that position.As I began to lose air, tears streamed down my face and my nose produced mucus.I wanted to beg him to stop, but I couldn't because my mouth was full of man cock.I tried desperately to inhale to get air into my lungs through my nostrils;However, the musky scent of his man bush was all I could inhale because my nose was pressed against his pubic hair.
Due to the fact that I was in excruciating pain and my jaw was now locked (I had to open them really wide due to the size of his wood), I thought I was going to faint at some point.When he abruptly began to grunt and seriously shiver, I had just begun to literally weep in frustration.His pole had crossed my throat, so the hot sperm went straight to my stomach.I was even denied the opportunity to taste his cum.
He withdrew his cock from my mouth after putting his valuables in my mouth bank, which made me desperately gasp for air.

He grumbled, "o boy na wha for you ohhhhh," frowning.

It sounded like a mashup of regret, disappointment, appreciation for a job well done, satisfaction, and guilt.

In the nearly pitch-black night, he undressed, stepped into the icy stream, and began his bath.My breath still smelt of sperm and a hint of weed as I remained seated.In order for us to depart together as is our custom, I waited for him to finish.He would only feel more guilty about what happened if left alone.

After he was done, he took me home on his tricycle with us both.

We never spoke to one another while we were riding.I said "good night" and added "we go see tomorrow" after he dropped me off.He turned around and continued on his own with a "no problem" response.

I had a good wank as soon as I got home.It was such a motivating thought to think about being nearly suffocated to death by a big dick.

The following day, Kufre and I met at the joint.Despite our best efforts not to look each other in the eye even in the midst of other people, he acted as though nothing had happened.

This continued for several days.

A few days later, I was with some guys at the joint, and they started to leave one by one.At last, there were only four of us left.Kufre, two other guys, and I.We should go to the neighborhood bar because one of the guys wanted to buy us all drinks.

Kufre made a rather suggestive throat clearing as I was about to accept the offer, and our eyes met.I immediately understood what he was getting at when his eyes appeared to say, "if you dare move from here..."The other two guys eventually left, leaving me and Kufre alone, so I turned down the offer.

As I sat quietly in the same place I had been the previous time, I could hear him playing Candy Crush on his phone.We remained silent for close to ten minutes.

I decided to join him and play games on my phone because I was bored.I pulled out my phone and started the game in a matter of seconds.Kufre spoke just as the intro music started playing. "You don't fear, don't you?You're here to answer the phone.He sounded so hostile, and this really scared me. "E be like you want me to scatter that phone on top of your head," he said.He carried on playing the game with his face fixed on his phone.This really perplexed me because his voice tone was more hostile than his facial expression, which was a very subtle frown.

I remained quiet and put my phone down gently.

He shuffled timidly toward me while still staring at his phone.I could see a small smirk on his face and a significant bulge in his floral-printed fitted short as he did so.

"You dey fear me, man? Why do you also fear?"He said this as he playedfully kicked my foot gently.

He began to slightly swing his upper torso like a shy child making a request with his now-full smirk.

"How far is it?He asked almost whisper-like.

I replied, "I dey o..."pretending to be unaware of what he was implying.To ensure that he would be the one to initiate everything this time, I had to act stupid.

The silence was strange.I could now clearly see the outline of his cock now.There was no doubt that his penis had become so turgid that it no longer resembled a large bulge;however, a raging dragon.

"How do you like to look?"He asked in a snide manner, his focus still fixed on the phone.
We were both aware that he was merely creating unnecessary drama to convey his horniness and cover up his message.
I replied, "am looking at what is in front of me."
He took a deep breath and exhaled loudly, exclaiming, "omoh....that your mouth ehhhh..."He moved his waist forward, a sign that he wanted me to pay attention to his cock.
"Who is this?"As I reached for his swollen penis, I inquired.
He chuckled, "na my AK 47."
I beguilingly requested, "make i see am."
He quickly turned off his phone, put it in his back pocket, and quickly unfastened his belt without wasting any time.His award-winning penis sprung out with agile joy as he took off his shorts.
I honestly felt as though I had just seen it for the first time.
It throbbed in my palms and felt so hot as I placed my hand over it.He pulled my head down on his enormous meat without warning, indicating that he wanted me to suck him, and I did as expected.
He asked huskily, "the other one sweet like this one?" as he pushed deeper into my stomach.
I withdrew my mouth from his cock and inquired as I was completely unsure of what I had heard.
He mumbled, "the back own" with an irritated frown. WHAT??????
Was my hearing accurate?
"BACK??????"
He hurriedly tore off his shirt, revealing his firm pacs and abs, and guided my head back to his penis after I had barely processed what he had said.
"I just want to know how e be," "I want to enter the other one."
He pushed into my mouth and groaned.
I was aware that Kufre acted impulsively.He has completely fallen in love with the new sexuality I've introduced him to, and he has complete faith in me.even though he was still having trouble accepting it.It could have ended our relationship if I refused to comply with him, especially now that he was independently manipulating the situation.He was the kind of person who preferred to be served in his own way.I was reluctant to begin describing roles to him;preferably not at that point.His agitated hormones were unable to process all of it.I had the idea of arranging a bottom for him, but the ominous look he gave me stopped me in my tracks and made me stop talking.In my hands, his penis began to quickly become limp.
I quickly informed him that I was joking and inquired if he had a lubricant with him.He asked if I had any after shaking his head;which I informed him I did not;except at home, where we hoped it would deter him.He told me to go home and get it while he waited for me, which disappointed me.
I could not continue my argument.He had won.
I went home after I left him.Because my dad was at home, I had to sneak into the hotel, force myself to use the bathroom to prevent accidents, wash up (punching my hole in the process), and get my grease before returning to slaughter.
I got there as it was already dark.The silhouette of Kufre's massive frame gave the impression that he was an entity, while the bushes gave the impression of ghosts.As I silently approached him, all that could be heard in the still night was the gentle gurgling of the stream.I had a deep

desire for him that was stronger than any sexual desire.I immediately followed suit because I could see that he was naked in the darkness.The cold night air made my skin no longer feel warm as I took off each piece of clothing.

I strode to him in the pitch-black with a tube of lube, now completely naked, and felt his icy body.Like silk on steel, his skin was firm and smooth.After our organs met, my erection started to move.I slowly embraced him and kissed his lips without asking.I begged him not to pull his face away, but he tried gently.I was in desperate need of him.He had to defame me from a place of deep connection if he wanted to, not just from a place of lustful thirst.

After a while, he parted his lips, then his teeth, and then our tongues merged in a divine dance as I continued to kiss him.His fingers lightly touched my naked waist, I felt.His grip on my waist got stronger as we kissed more.He held me so tightly and gave me a kiss that only a lover would give.I put some lubricant in my hands, which were resting on his solid shoulders, and rubbed them in between my thighs as we looked into each other's mouths.I slowly slid my moistened in-between thighs on his fuck pole after moving my waist back enough to ensure that his long, fat cock was correctly aimed at me.The sensation made him exhale.He cherished it. As soon as he started happily fucking my thighs, his kissing got stronger.As I guided his hands to my fleshy plum bum, which many guys, including straight men, are disappointed that I wasn't bottom, I lubricated my ass hole.As he continued to deep kiss me and fuck my thighs, he greedily grabbed my ass.My pucker hole was found by one of his fingers;His finger moved in the same avarice as his kiss and thrust.

He stuck his finger so deeply into me that it felt like he was looking for treasures that had been lost.My rectum began secreting fluids that made it so slippery like a wet vagina after some time of his probing.Although the kissing was just too magical for my brain to fully register everything that was happening, I began to feel sharp pains in my ass.But at one point, I had to force myself to feel what was going on in my ass with my hands alongside Kufre's finger, and what I found truly scared me.

I had four fingers stuck in my hole!!!!!!

I started to panic at that point.I tried to remove his hands by grabbing his wrist;However, he abruptly whispered, "Relax," and nudged me away.I also did.

In the same rhythm as he was fucking my thighs, he started jabbing his fingers into my hole. In a single swift swing, he turned me around and started fucking my thighs from behind, occasionally teasing my hole with his dick head.He would push his cock deeper into my cunt every time he teased my hole with his crude head.He kept doing this until he could only get his dingy head through my ass hole.

(Despite the fact that he fucked me with four fingers, his dick was still too big to enter the room)After a brief pause, his cocked head still in my ass hole corridor, he began to slowly whine his waist clockwise and anticlockwise.Because it was so painful, I asked him to hold on while I generously applied more lube to my ass and his heavy pole.It hurt less when he tried to get back inside of me.

He was able to get his tool into my groin gradually.

He moaned in my ear, "you are very sweet," as he drove the final inch into my stomach.I felt as though I had swallowed a young goat.I was so stuffed.My dick started to get so hard as he started to thrust that it felt like it was going to break apart.The feeling I had is beyond my ability to describe.I only knew that I moaned and begged him to fuck me;which he continued to

respond with, "yah baby...yah baby....yah baby..." I started wanking my cock out of frustration because the erection was severely hurting my dick.I screamed so loudly while Kufre rode me on his powerful horse that he had to wrap his large hand around my mouth to drown it out.
He began to jerk, whimper, and groan in muffled falsetto as soon as I began to feel my cum shoot out of my dick hole.As he once more poured everything into my stomach, I could only feel his cock pulse several times on my rectum.He continued to thrust for approximately three more minutes before his cock became soft.
I embraced and kissed him as he removed his cock from me.He did not pause.As he put his finger in the now-wide open cum dump hole, he gave a positive response.
He asked, "Hope say you no wound?" as we exited the stream.
I told him fine with a smile.
When I inquired about his enjoyment, he responded, "omoh ehhhh......i don't die finish."
Even though it's been more than eight months since this happened, I still can't imagine Kufre topping me.

9 798359 421782